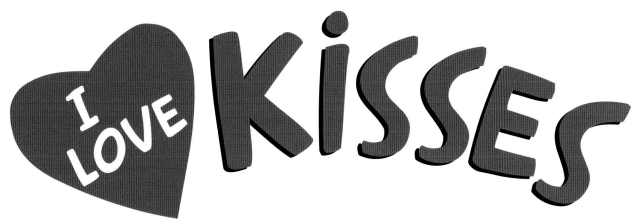

I LOVE KISSES

Sheryl McFarlane
Brenna Vaughan

sourcebooks
jabberwocky

Published by Sourcebooks Jabberwocky, an imprint of
Sourcebooks, Inc.
P.O. Box 4410, Naperville, Illinois 60567–4410
(630) 961–3900
Fax: (630) 961–2168
sourcebooks.com

Library of Congress Cataloging-in-Publication data is on file with the publisher.

Source of Production: Oceanic Graphic Printing, Kowloon, Hong Kong, China
Date of Production: October 2017
Run Number: 5010335

Printed and bound in China.
OGP 10 9 8 7 6 5 4 3 2 1

For all the moms, dads, and caregivers who
shower our little ones with kisses and love.
—*S. M.*

For my kissable Tobey and Ava.
—*B. V.*

I love kisses.
I'll bet that you do too!

"Wake up, sleepyhead" kisses

Raspberry jam and bread kisses

Sloppy licking pup kisses

Jungle gym climb up kisses

Baby brother drool kisses

Splashing in the pool kisses

Stung by a bee kisses

"Ouch, I scraped my knee!" kisses

Noisy tambourine kisses

Ghostly Halloween kisses

Sticky little sister kisses

Scratchy-
tongued
Mister
kisses

"I'm sorry
that you're sad!"
kisses

Mom can't
stay mad
kisses

Now it's time
to go kisses

Valentine's Day
glow kisses

Lipstick on my
cheek kisses

"Found you!"
hide-and-seek
kisses

Auntie's pretend air kisses

Daddy's prickly hair kisses

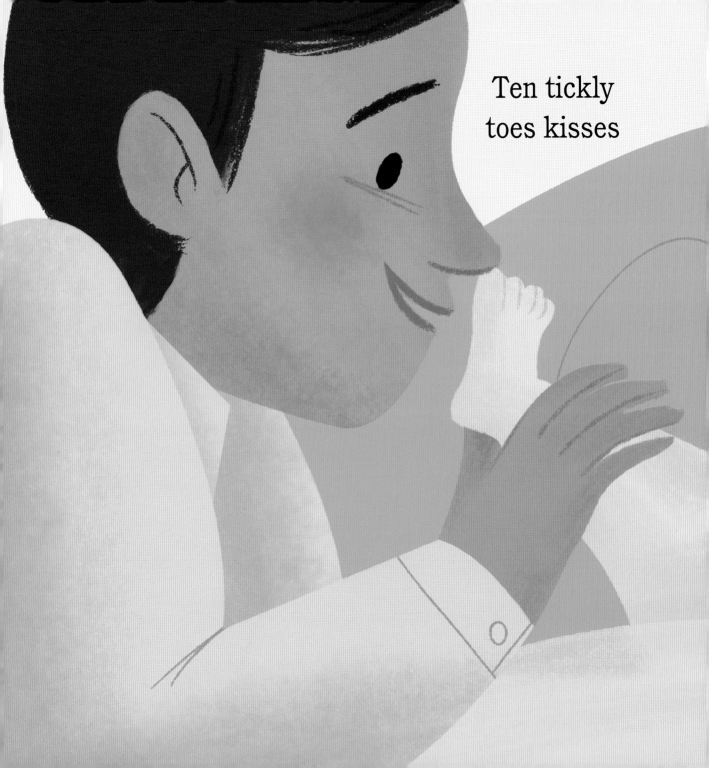

Ten tickly
toes kisses

Two snuggly
nose kisses

"Bedtime already?" kisses

Cuddle up
with teddy
kisses.

But the very best kisses

are the ones I get from you.

About the Author

Sheryl McFarlane has written fourteen books for kids and teens and has won the Moonbeam Award for YA in the U.S. She's worked for the Canadian Children's Book Center and has served on multiple award committees.

About the Illustrator

Brenna Vaughan has her BFA in illustration from the Memphis College of Art. She lives in St. Louis, Missouri.